W9-DGO-997

Tip and Tucker

Road Trip

Words by **Ann Ingalls** and **Sue Lowell Gallion**

Pictures by André Ceolin

PUBLISHED BY SLEEPING BEAR PRESS

For Ben and Jackson
—Sue

For Stella and Sadie
—Ann

To Gabriel and Grace, for their patience and support
—André

Text Copyright © 2019 Ann Ingalls and Sue Lowell Gallion
Illustration Copyright © 2019 André Ceolin
Design Copyright © 2019 Sleeping Bear Press

Sleeping Bear Press™
2395 South Huron Parkway, Suite 200
Ann Arbor, MI 48104
www.sleepingbearpress.com
© Sleeping Bear Press

Printed and bound in the United States.
10 9 8 7 6 5 4 3 2 1
Library of Congress Cataloging-in-Publication Data
Names: Ingalls, Ann, author. | Gallion, Sue Lowell, author. | Ceolin, Andre, illustrator.
Title: Road trip! / written by Ann Ingalls and Sue Lowell Gallion ; illustrated by Andre Ceolin.
Description: Ann Arbor, MI : Sleeping Bear Press, [2019] | Series: Tip and Tucker ; book 1 |
Summary: Two hamsters, one named Tip and the other Tucker, one fearful and one fearless,
are purchased from a pet store by Mr. Lopez for his classroom.
Identifiers: LCCN 2018037165
ISBN 9781534110069 (hardcover)
ISBN 9781534110076 (pbk.)
Subjects: | CYAC: Hamsters—Fiction. | Teachers—Fiction. | Hispanic Americans—Fiction.
Classification: LCC PZ7.I45 Ro 2019 | DDC [E]—dc23
LC record available at https://lccn.loc.gov/2018037165

Mr. Lopez opens the door.
He walks in the store.
Tucker pops up.
Up to the top of his home.

Who could it be?

Tucker spins on his wheel to see.

A parrot? *No.*

A puppy? *No.*

A snake? *No.*

Tucker likes new things.

"Hi, Mr. Lopez," says Rosa.

"Hi, Rosa," says Mr. Lopez.

Mr. Lopez has brown eyes.

He has black glasses and a big smile.

"Tip!" says Tucker. "Come and see!"

Tip peeks.

He sees a big nose.

Big brown eyes.

Big black glasses.

Blink. Blink.

"Oh no," says Tip.
He hides in his igloo.
Just the tip of his tail shows.

"I want those two," says Mr. Lopez.
"Do you need a cage?" Rosa asks.
"And food?"
"Yes," says Mr. Lopez.

"A new home for them," says Rosa.
"It will be noisy," says Mr. Lopez.
"But it will be fun!"

"A *noisy* new home?" says Tip.
Tip does not like noisy things.

Noisy parrots.
Bawk. Bawk.

Noisy puppies.
Bark! Bark!

"Who is this?" asks Mr. Lopez.
"The little one is Tip," says Rosa.
"The fuzzy one is Tucker."

Tucker sniffs.
Sniff. Sniff. Sniff.
He likes new things.

"¡*Vamos!*" Mr. Lopez says.
"Let's go!"
Then the cage jumps.
The cage bumps!
Tip flips.
Tucker flops.

"Where are we going?" Tip says.
"We are flying!" says Tucker.
"To the noisy new home!"

Out goes Mr. Lopez.
Out into the sun.
Tip and Tucker blink.

Mr. Lopez opens the car door.

He sets the cage on some books.

Tucker's nose twitches.

Sniff. Sniff. Sniff

"I smell coffee," says Tip.
"I smell fries," says Tucker.
"I like those smells!"

"But I am scared," says Tip.
"Do not worry," says Tucker.
Tip hides.
Just the tip of his tail shows.

The car bumps. The cage jumps.
The car zips. The car zigs.
The car stops.

Mr. Lopez picks up the cage.
Step. Step. Step.
Mr. Lopez walks to a building.
Snap. He unlocks a door.

Click. Click. Click.

Mr. Lopez walks down a hall.

Creak. He opens a new door.

Clunk! The cage bumps.

Tucker sniffs.
He looks.
Bins full of blocks.
Jump ropes and balls.
Books everywhere.

Tucker likes this new place.
"Tip, come out!" he says.
Tip peeks.

Mr. Lopez looks at Tip.
He looks at Tucker.
He smiles.
"*Hasta mañana*," says Mr. Lopez.
"See you tomorrow.
Your first day of school!"

Out go the lights.
Out goes Mr. Lopez.
Tip goes into his igloo.

"What is school?" asks Tip in a tiny voice.
"I don't know," says Tucker.
His voice is tiny too.
"But we will find out together."